Melpomene, Edited by Gwendolyn Taunton © 2012, ©Numen Books 2012

The copyright of content is retained by the authors.

Published by Numen Books, 2012

ISBN 978-0-9871581-5-4

# Melpomene

Him, O Melpomene, upon whom at his birth thou hast once looked with favouring eye, the Isthmian contest shall not render eminent as a wrestler; the swift horse shall not draw him triumphant in a Grecian car; nor shall warlike achievement show him in the Capitol, a general adorned with the Delian laurel, on account of his having quashed the proud threats of kings: but such waters as flow through the fertile Tiber, and the dense leaves of the groves, shall make him distinguished by the Aeolian verse. The sons of Rome, the queen of cities, deign to rank me among the amiable band of poets; and now I am less carped at by the tooth of envy. O muse, regulating the harmony of the gilded shell! O thou, who canst immediately bestow, if thou please, the notes of the swan upon the mute fish! It is entirely by thy gift that I am marked out, as the stringer of the Roman lyre, by the fingers of passengers; that I breathe, and give pleasure (if I give pleasure), is yours.

*- The Fourth Book of the Odes of Horace*

# Contents

## Liber Veneficium

## Liber Maeroris

# Liber Fatum

# Liber Mortuorum

# Liber Veneficium

# Melpomene

## The Spiritual Dawn

Charles Baudelaire

When the morning white and rosy breaks,
With the gnawing Ideal, upon the debauchee,
By the power of a strange decree,
Within the sotted beast an Angel wakes.

The mental Heaven's inaccessible blue,
For wearied mortals that still dream and mourn,
Expands and sinks; towards the chasm drawn.
Thus, cherished goddess, Being pure and true—

Upon the rests of foolish orgy-nights
Thine image, more sublime, more pink, more clear,
Before my staring eyes is ever there.

The sun has darkened all the candle lights;
And thus thy spectre like the immortal sun,
Is ever victorious—thou resplendent one!

# Melpomene

## Dream-Land

### Edgar Allan Poe

BY a route obscure and lonely,
Haunted by ill angels only,
Where an Eidolon, named NIGHT,
On a black throne reigns upright,
I have reached these lands but newly
From an ultimate dim Thule—
From a wild weird clime that lieth, sublime,
Out of SPACE—out of TIME.

Bottomless vales and boundless floods,
And chasms, and caves, and Titian woods,
With forms that no man can discover
For the dews that drip all over;
Mountains toppling evermore
Into seas without a shore;
Seas that restlessly aspire,
Surging, unto skies of fire;
Lakes that endlessly outspread
Their lone waters—lone and dead,—
Their still waters—still and chilly
With the snows of the lolling lily.

By the lakes that thus outspread
Their lone waters, lone and dead,—
Their sad waters, sad and chilly

# Melpomene

With the snows of the lolling lily,—
By the mountains—near the river
Murmuring lowly, murmuring ever,—
By the grey woods,—by the swamp
Where the toad and the newt encamp,—
By the dismal tarns and pools
Where dwell the Ghouls,—
By each spot the most unholy—
In each nook most melancholy,—
There the traveller meets aghast
Sheeted Memories of the Past—
Shrouded forms that start and sigh
As they pass the wanderer by—
White-robed forms of friends long given,
In agony, to the Earth—and Heaven.

For the heart whose woes are legion
'Tis a peaceful, soothing region—
For the spirit that walks in shadow
'Tis—oh 'tis an Eldorado!
But the traveller, travelling through it,
May not—dare not openly view it;
Never its mysteries are exposed
To the weak human eye unclosed;
So wills its King, who hath forbid
The uplifting of the fringed lid;
And thus the sad Soul that here passes
Beholds it but through darkened glasses.

# Melpomene

By a route obscure and lonely,
Haunted by ill angels only,
Where an Eidolon, named NIGHT,
On a black throne reigns upright,
I have wandered home but newly
From this ultimate dim Thule.

# Melpomene

## Apotheosis.

Emily Dickinson

Come slowly, Eden!
Lips unused to thee,
Bashful, sip thy jasmines,
As the fainting bee,

Reaching late his flower,
Round her chamber hums,
Counts his nectars — enters,
And is lost in balms!

## The Human Abstract

### William Blake

Pity would be no more
If we did not make somebody poor,
And Mercy no more could be
If all were as happy as we.
And mutual fear brings Peace,
Till the selfish loves increase;
Then Cruelty knits a snare,
And spreads his baits with care.

He sits down with his holy fears,
And waters the ground with tears;
Then Humility takes its root
Underneath his foot.

Soon spreads the dismal shade
Of Mystery over his head,
And the caterpillar and fly
Feed on the Mystery.

And it bears the fruit of Deceit,
Ruddy and sweet to eat,
And the raven his nest has made
In its thickest shade.

The gods of the earth and sea
Sought through nature to find this tree,

# Melpomene

But their search was all in vain:
There grows one in the human Brain.

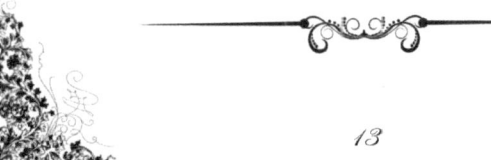

# Melpomene

## The Bricklayer

Math Jones

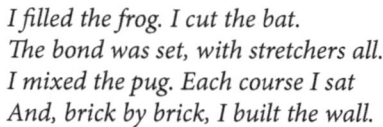

> I filled the frog. I cut the bat.
> The bond was set, with stretchers all.
> I mixed the pug. Each course I sat
> And, brick by brick, I built the wall.

They called her witch, though none could prove,
So burning would not be her doom -
For sure, she'd had the friar's love:
It was his pup within her womb.

It was his seed, and so he hung,
And all were pleased to see his fall,
But she into a vault was flung,
To be bricked up behind a wall.

>> Stripped of wimple she was brung
>> And never spoke a word at all.

T'was I was called with trowel and hod,
With lime-cut sand and plaster mix,
Whilst Abbot sang his curse to God,
To seal her fate with red clay bricks.

Beaten blue, in stained chemise,
She huddled, wrapped her arms around
Her belly swelling; bloody knees

# Melpomene

And shattered ankles on the ground.

In hope, God's anger to appease,
She whispered prayers without a sound

A witch she was, the Abbot swore,
A demon's lover, loose and wild,
But none should stain their soul before
Their God, by slaying of a child,

And none with blood should stain their hand,
Or smirch their name with such a kind;
The justice of the Lord's command
Demanded she must be confined,

Forever from man's consort banned,
Alone and to her fate consigned.

*I filled the frog. I cut the bat.*
*The bond was set, with stretchers all.*
*I mixed the pug. Each course I sat*
*And, brick by brick, I built the wall.*

Seven years my master served
And seven years a journeyman,
My courage by her plight unnerved,
My hand remained a steady span,
And seven years a master, I
Maintained a true and steady pace

# Melpomene

In laying brick and mortar high
To hide a shamed and lowing face.

With calloused hands and shoulders broad,
I sealed that woman in the place.

I bedded in each brick by turn,
As if a home or guarding wall
Were my commission: fee well earned,
Centuries standing, never fall;

And all the while her silent plea
Came seeping through the fired clay,
Reverberated soundlessly
From every muting brick I lay,

Nor ceased until the wall was done,
That stole from her the light of day,

*I filled the frog. I cut the bat.*
*The bond was set, with stretchers all.*
*I mixed the pug. Each course I sat*
*And, brick by brick, I built the wall.*

The bond complete, I turned away
And only darkness could I see,
A thousand granite shades of grey,
A world of stone enclosing me.

# Melpomene

The wall complete, I turned again,
As water into sand immersed,
As if with mortar bedded in;
The church's blessing in my purse.

> Indulgences to clear my sin,
> Far heavier than any curse.

In deepest, all-encasing night,
My wife beside me, soundly fed,
As cold as stone, as hard as fright,
I lie like brick within my bed

And seek to wall her from my sight,
Else wish that it were I instead.

> And over me and all around,
> In courses fair and smoothly laid,
> Brick on brick, my feeling to surround,
> The vault that I my prison made.

> The vault where I might lay me down,
> By my most holy priest betrayed.

*I filled the frog. I cut the bat.*
*The bond was set, with stretchers all.*
*I mixed the pug. Each course I sat*
*And, brick by brick, I built the wall.*

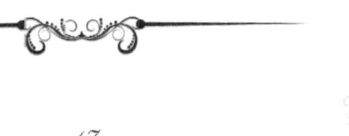

# Melpomene

They found me at the dawn of day,
A twelve month after, by the wall:
Scratched fingermarks dug in the clay,
No fingers left, nor life. But all
May see me still, at night, they say,
Screaming madly down the hall.

And all may see the Abbot's skull,
Found buried 'neath his private cell,
With lime-cut sand and plaster full
As if in mortar he had fell;

As if his keen and pious soul
Were here bricked up with me in Hell.

# Melpomene

## Wulfs Schädel

Bill Noble

I wandered stricken
Had she enchanted my mead?
Through the dewy forest
Under overcast skies
Confusion before my eyes
As birds reluctantly chorused
My sweat did stickily bead
And the air seemed to thicken

I came across a dolmen
It soared athwart my face.
I brushed moss and spiderwebs
In horror, and tasted loamy soil
I felt the hands of others toil
As each present moment ebbs
Yea, the hands were of that race
Which ruled before the Roman.

*What determined hands worked*
*These hard and rough stones!*
*Shaping each menhir rudely*
*To fit its nearest brother;*
*Each supporting one another;*
*And not so more finely than less crudely*
*Were a legion of jagged runes -*
*But what above them lurked*

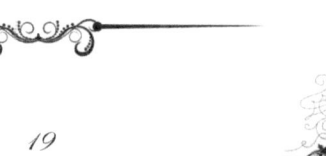

# Melpomene

Set into a cleft in the stone
Almost hidden by grey moss
Gripped my heart with terror
And bade me not to shift
My feet I could not lift
Thoughts of motion seemed in error;
But what caused this loss?
A grim snout of tooth and bone.

Once, eons past, this face
Held eyes and ears of cunning
A fiery spark of awareness
And warm pulse of blood's flow
But what passion it did know
Has passed; in all fairness
I would have been running,
If he yet lived, from this place.

His passion has passed
And his heart fell still
First his lips cooled
Then they turned to dust
He let go of the lust
By which power he ruled
Which drove him to each kill
As he hunted his realm vast.

And all that remains there
Is this tired old visage,

# *Melpomene*

Delicate and fey
And devoid of certain life
Seeming free from all strife
Or need to stalk prey
Yet still like some mirage
That face seemed to stare.

I gaped, but no sound could toll
While my heart cried its fear
And stared on and on
Into hollow eye sockets
Long-emptied pockets
Whose orbs had long been gone
Yet still seemed to leer
Into the pit of my soul

She found me there
Prone on the mossy glade
Blood scabbing on my scraped cheeks
My fingernails broken
And I have not spoken
For three whole weeks
Because I am afraid
Her throat I might tear

If I give in
To the beautiful promise
Of Fenris:
"Your soul be set free."

# *Melpomene*

*This must not be -*
*That I might feel no remorse*
*When I compromise*
*The living*

But he told me
My name was Wulfsherz
And I was his brother
And he pitied my travesty
Locked in the fey body
Of a degenerate ape
And he told me "Escape!"
"Kill, and be free!"

And I thought: No
But I was silent
For I feared a great howl
And my cage is my comfort

How I envy that dead beast's dust!

# Melpomene

## The Love Potion

Math Jones

The alchemist, by thick and studied walls defenced,
Despaired; all golden days and leaden nights he gave,
His pool of years evaporated and condensed,
To find a potent brew could bring him back to love.

A potion true and shining clear as living quartz,
In anguish he besought, his stony heart to heal;
And lab'ring 'neath his crucible and sharp retorts
Was simple Sofia, his bed-thing and make-meal.

His plan was plain, to constitute a loving cup
Of liquor from the recipes of olden lore,
Imbuing in each steaming brew for him to sup,
A morsel of the women come to him for cure.

From each and every beauty he would snatch a trace
Of skin, of spit, or hair, or filed nail dispensed,
To fortify his potion; dreaming on that face
The drink, he hoped, on her would leave his heart
incensed.

The recipe was true, th'ingredients fine and good.
The potion was well brewed, with practice surely made,
But though a short time, his heart burgeoned as it should,
Each girl would show some imperfection; love would

23

fade.
And no solution could he find to why his hope was so
betrayed.
 Sofia was simple but studied in his ways,
And looked on him with youthful love more natural
grown;
For he was kind upon his better, hopeful days,
And mercy, in her deepest poverty, had shown.

She had no skill to read, nor wit to alchemise,
Nor wish to see him win a lady's marriage band.
A strategy she worked and so, behind his eyes,
Into each fresh-made potion dropped a grain of sand.

So consequently, each new flaring spark of care,
Each new struck match, would not a lasting flame ignite,
But some love-quenching, niggling quibble would impair
His passion, leave the lady worthless in his sight.

On these days cruel, he left Sofia bruised in bed,
To grind with pestle, calcifying, bitter grown,
Till some fresh maiden lifted up once more his head,
Then sweeter grew his humour; kindness she was shown.

Full sore with love, to his alembic, sly she crept
With silent steps; to spoil his newest broth she inched
His sleeping body by; he watched her as she stepped,
The smallest speck of sand within her finger pinched.

## Melpomene

Before him screamed the truth, the answer to his care,

The saboteur of all his dreams, whose love had torn
The vision from his tearful eye; right then and there,
He killed her dead, and buried her before the morn.
He killed her cold, discarded her and wished her never
born.

At Evensong, to drain the unspoilt drink he came,
For one time free of sand; once more his heart did swell,
And burn and burst! He fell and called his lover's name;
Felt grief more keen than sharpest pen has means to tell.

No grieving, mournful, heart-broke lover ever loved so
well -
Into his cup a drop of sweet Sofia's blood had fell.

# Melpomene

## Dark Lord of Abussos

### Bernardo Sena

Abandon hope all ye who pass through those polar wastelands of the southern-most desolate terra ignota. There where one finds looming in the extent of darkness the great Mount Erebus. O wandering stranger into those barren and destitute landscapes of the ice-covered lands. A lonesome place where for half a yearly cycle, light will not shine. Erebus, how it stands poised in its own imposing manner, piercing the crystalline-dark sky of the eternal night, dotted with the glimmer of distant dying stars. Therein residing in that behemoth monstrosity, the Dark Lord of the Abussos remains, hidden from the known world, it is there that he lays waiting for when to unleash the open maw of those greater depths of the abyss...

The shadow of darkness begins to slither across the sombre room... A body of anatomy... adorned in the blackest of vestments, lain upon a white, marble, embalming table – wherefore the blackest of blood doth drip from his pores, collected by the grooves that surround the table's periphery, leading down towards the floor and streaming across to the room's contour into each corner. There it flows down into an unseen gutter to the bowels of some unknown underworld. That grotesque image stares back in silence, the skull-like deathmask covering his face slightly shifts as he stirs from the Dreaming. There he doth slumber for a cycle of six seasons, when the light conquers the ice-ridden domain. And now, from those very depths of his deep

sleep, he shall be awakened by the transition of the earthly sphere in its cosmic revolution, the latter half of the yearly cycle begins, and darkness shall now reign for six seasons yonder... There in the desolate Antarctic, a white chaos of fog and ice surrounding every which way.

Behold! That very demon, nay more than demon but some unforetold ancient god, an entity far surpassing the horrors of one's imagination.... Yes, that presence now stands by the intermediate plane, at gateway of Fatum, for it is not your worst nightmare come to life, alas no! It is but a stark reminder of that tarnished past you have forgotten. Writhing, crawling, gestating, festering, squirming in embryonic anguish, incarnate. Waiting to take hold once more. It is that aspect you choose to ignore in fear, to relinquish upon the abyss of memory altogether. It thrives upon the chaos you now drown out... Now it becomes reborn to conquer that undying soul. The gates to that very "Hell" you fear the most will be flung wide open in retribution, to unleash those ancient "abominations" who were once revered as true gods, imprisoned by the wretched guardian of light. The distant cries out from the Darkness emerge as the world now recoils.

He rises from that deep slumber, lifting himself off his bed of marble, observing around him. There he looks to the shadow-play dancing across the glacial walls of his ice fortress, hearing the eerie instrumental music that permeates throughout. From beyond he can hear the

horns sounding off... at this he moves towards his macro-telescopic viewing device. The lens to which protrudes out of the crystal-mirror large window of his room. Peering out he observes the revelrous trampling of an army of snow-covered corpses, revenants even, all shambling from beneath the ground and clambering over each other in a menagerie of madness towards the great mountain of his dominion, he, the Dark Lord. Those creatures have grown restless, from their frozen and ancient graves, risen forth to embark on their passage – to return to the glorious oblivion that awaits their destiny. And he the Dark Lord, shall be the harbinger of their abysmal release.

The Dark Lord turns away from his viewing device to follow the faint hum of the eerie, instrumental music through to a blackened doorway. He follows his shadow's footsteps into a grandiose hall, covered in a checkerboard floor, whereupon the Shadows out of Time and Space conjure a terrifying performance and dance, interloping to and fro to the music that now emanates from some invisible point in the middle of the grand hall. The shard of gray light pierces the grand hall from up above, the last remnants of the twilight. He passes through the middle, taking a methodical step upon each square, black then white... then black again before white. As he passes through the room the Shadows disperse, however continuing their obscure dance, and the music heightens to a deafening roar. And as that music carries on its gruesome symphony the words out of nowhere can be heard, a utterance of sorts repeating

itself...

"In the night, in the dark... no one will hear you. No one will come. You are all alone, in thought and in those shadows of your own doubt. Only the unmentionable terrors that dwell therein will draw near, with every breath taken. They surely will have such sights to show you... for the Dark Lord has risen and shall unveil the great portal."
As this cacophony plays out, the Dark Lord seats himself upon a throne made of frosted bones. Behind that the portal lays, an open maw of deep blackness, that vortex of nothingness, oblivion lays therein. Darkness propels forward from within, spilling outward ever so gradually. He sits there and gazes through the spectrum. All is ready. He turns his head upwards and there the stars glisten with such brilliance to one side of the pitch-black sky, on the other side the aurora australis billows in ribbons creating a whirl of evocative coloration.

Now, as the earth declines unto itself in decay, the Darkness takes hold manifesting atop putrefaction. Purging towards a renewed purification. The world is delivered once more through the journey into oblivion. The Shadows out of Time and Space prevail more intensely, ever watchful to the drama played out by the dance of Death. A definitive horror pierces the very mortal soul throughout the hours of day, setting a deep unease and melancholy of our human condition upon this earthly realm.

# *Melpomene*

This is the Great Fall into Abussos. Prepare, or you shall fully disappear and never return again.

# Melpomene

---

## A Raven In The Throat Of Analogies

*J. Karl Bogartte*

To be transparent encloses the world in transparency, extending lucid dreams. Adopted crystal of wind, welding light to breath, wind with it's lightning in the house of cranes keeps you alive, by accident… for an accidental glance, in a passage by stars. Windows in the dead of night, exposing presence without warning. Mirrors with their wings. When you sleep it is in the photograph. A supernatural riverbed.

*

The acidity of lunar nitrates, your measure, disoriented navigation, severe as her blackened animal mouth dripping into yearning, a moving silk, waterfall desiring the measure of stone. There is only dusk following the travelers with their nets. A great roaring of astrological cabinets dragged by horses in mirrors witnessed by chimera in old films deteriorating in warehouses. A history of unruly kisses promising madness in ancient Greek letters reflecting the nearness of infinity.

*

Her body is silence hallucinating, sipping the hot wax of a feverish dive, swallowing the scent in pursuit of her image, your image, a ravaging in your hearsay and mirrored reversal. An initiated innocence distilled in the Calat of a witch-faced al 'Ambra, fiddling with optics to arouse

liquids from her swollen lips, swirling all the sighs in your mouth. Bursting seeds, eggs forced open, starlight written in blood, in the body, for the sea... The simultaneous computations among strangers.

*

Awareness is the siege of lightning wired to other more diversionary implements as rare and beautiful as a nameless girl lost in her mother's dark machinery. She shivers on the scale of wonder and terror, cherished ash, retching black moonlight. Writing her name numerous times to anticipate the clarity of sudden sparks, there is only the whisper of sure bets placed in tandem with time being in her space, the purity of disrespect, a disruptive intimacy releasing the black gloves of a harbor flourishing underground.

*

"Turbulence, my love, makes your beauty eternal, like the sea when it sleeps, like the cistern when it overflows, like the moon..." when it litters the city with long-haired armatures, resembling distant relatives and sudden waifs, where the lock-maker's dust on the window illuminates the riddles where natural elements gather to enfilade... where light waits in ambush for the morning to approach, like a wound that provokes the landscape into internal bleeding and vanishing.

# *Melpomene*

*

She has the hair of alcheringa and aisling, the soft Huron, in the sparkling of the amps and the antlers fallen, releasing warmth that speaks and shakes, and moves the earth into grooming. Her shore fevers, purloined with the joy of absence, wave-struck, with skeletal emanations polishing moths into fortune-tellers. Oxidation and crystallization empower a solarized splendor (as mimicry), just before rushing out to strangle it and shape it into furious portals. "For the wick that shares your eyes with voices, aligned, Aleya, Púca, Vilya, Min Min, Wii'ipay and the corpse candles of a sudden vivisection... And those who glow, bleeding radiance, breeding in spirals, pounding on the rocks."

*

After the lighthouse there were endless nights and living rooms fraught with constellations and cries of northern lights. The reindeer princess gestating in the anti-myth of what cannot be seen, mutations of a drift out of consciousness. In permutation... she is spawning. The lower half of the Ω stakes a claim in the rich cochineal and silver of prehistoric bookmaking. At midnight the piano tuner places a winning number in the wrong hands. The hero and heroine refuse to agree, setting anarchy into motion with the moonlight of misplaced eyeglasses. Wandering becomes an art of disagreement. In accord...

*Melpomene*

\*

The wise man is the pitchfork of circles triggering a garden. The sorrow of Ithaca automatically combs out her tremulous locks. There are courtyards guarding the remnants of bliss, *"such a terrifyingly effortless flow..."* Light moves in close to the rattling of stamen, sliding into a gusset of bees. The image of alignment tears nebulae in the fabric. Lovers, foaming at the mouth. For each candle lit and dipped, and whipped into a distraught pool of eager pyramids, there is that irreversible moment of no return.

\*

Light and dark, by distinction severed from kinship and wreck, struck a bargain between themselves, she crafting that which becomes her shimmer, and he more alive than his tales, risking presence. The heaviness of tusk, swinging by forest limbs, the thrust of a ship's luminous bone, twice fount and clone. "Such awful weight astounds, sinking beyond relief. I come to you as carnal root and distraught awkward delight. I am against. I am negative and dangerous bright. I am your trance and diligent gate... I am dawn's desperate breeding. And I am frightfully unfinished..."

\*

The voyeurs are a gathering of the sea, a desolation spinning its wheels, pulling its gravity inwards. Neither moral

# Melpomene

nor immoral, but a vicarious enchantment of motion, intuitive and fixed gyroscope, womanly as fire, elemental consciousness slipping from hand to hand. A visionary loom throwing sparks into the first arc of a monumental alibi printing in the dark... Winds where there were bones, rain where flesh was hidden. Shadow where extinguishing lights are hammered into the color of eyes risking a final exposure.

\*

"*The wind, leopard...*" "*The rain, assassin...*" The book, sister to the bell-tower, gathering steam, remote from the forest, burnt by moonlight into a long-limbed calyx that spins around in circles, repeating your name, a coupling of numbers, kissing only water, savage computations. Shadowboxing with consciousness. Life is that breath of Jívaro dust blown into the face. A clockwork scent drawing blood, where indigo climbs into darkness. Crushed into light.

\*

Fire seduces water and invents new pleasures for its landscape, raising pinnacles out of intoxication. The anther region of your expectations is a harrowing sorcery invoking the self-image, the reverse of identity, an ecstasy of conjuring that doubles as a portrait, a trilogy, the arrow of potentiality passing through its target. A cluster of left-

handed spores and a tincture of departure, the residing instinct of carnal ridges, humming, a starless body, papyri of missing limbs, articulating in darkness.

*

A gathering of elders, the morning ones, the flawed-into-evening ones, the scatter of stars in leopard's flame, in the snarl, in the palpitation of an empty street, in the sunstroke of word-swallowing, life is a prowling movement, motionless between analogies, a fusion of images. The Sovereign Enigma, after the rain, is self-suspended in the nascent suspicion of a stranger at the door of uncertain presence... She abuses the circle... Her curious horn attracts latent desires... She can be found spawning there where the Northern Lights enter your body to breathe, into a prism.

*

Slender measurements like sudden changes in weather. Each moan and hiss slowly extricated according to the lineaments of time and space, daughter-shaped, emerging, shedding appearance. No one is moving. Being, meanwhile, is antagonistic and decidedly ambiguous. You are sleeping in tunnels. Posing as a biological morning. Threadbare. Taunting. Annotated vicariously in the black ink of a sequence of irresistible and dangerous subliminal activating devices. Words stuck in sap, impregnated by

prurient suggestions. The pages smeared with poisons, hallucinogens, concealed weapons. The exhalation of animal psychology spreading out into space.

\*

When it becomes imperative to disbelieve and approach the flood, by swindling the distance in the tillering of unthinkable conspiracy, who you are matters less than the scheme of outdoing yourself, being undone. You become profound with light in the secret of the craving. Become a language outside the body, scrambling in the dark landscape that colors the body, windows it – cauterized in your shadowing.

\*

The enchanted liquors of Hagar Qim defining the sutures of a collapse into ambiguous space, are camouflaged by thirst and the horns of the hunt, your italics, the focus, the bride armed, the leap into sparks. Animal solutions swirled in peripheral bedchambers tilting against the modus operandi of escaping with life intact and fusing in the wings, forked and illumined...

\*

The awkward history of attraction approaches a sinister chemistry in a daring ceremony of glances. The act of

waking up is whipped into a frenzy of invisibility, to trick the sphinx into firing up her veils. The object is the mane convulsing and the unfixing of motion, intruding on the past, on another night of higher frequency. Life is an aching pause between transparency and a wall with no stone unturned, merely a glimpse, yet darker still, a lake-faced over-saturated luminosity of rapid breathing. Silence convenes in another body whispering poppies.

*

Who sees night brightly striking threads? Igniting gestures, presence divided by light, watching the face that sees itself from behind... in the place of magnetic landscapes drawn into elaborate circles, into portraits and original movement, who captivates the crossing, through the edges, grinding to a halt in midstream... Not seeing with the eyes. As viewed by the voyeurs who finish it...

# Melpomene

## No Time Like Infinity

Bernardo Sena

Do you know who you were?
Remember the sands of time
A place forgotten in-between
Left you in limbo and isolation

Take a look behind you
Follow the path of your shadow
Counter-parts exist all around
That ego, your worst enemy...

...Your own kind that you know
Live without love, and no one
Loves THEIR life, and assume nothing
Changes occur every which way

The dawn opens up a gateway
Escape into the next dimension
Awareness has just begun
It's all just a step away

Darkness clouds your memory
Tomorrow it will all be a dream
Then that which you knew nevermore
And everyone will go the same

Space is a place I want to disappear

# Melpomene

Time is a measure to bend at will
Knowledge is finite as long as you think
Power can be obtained by corruption

Leave your cloak at the doorway
The elder gods will be here soon
Take you away to the shores of destiny
The thread of the circle begins to unravel

...

The circle does not begins nor does it end.
It is maintained by the source of everything holding it
together in place by the illustrious illusion, incurred by the
infinite ignorance of the manmade construct.

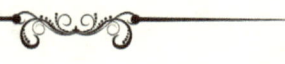

# Melpomene

---

## The Book of Thel

William Blake

THEL

I

The daughters of Mne Seraphim led round their sunny flocks,
All but the youngest: she in paleness sought the secret air.
To fade away like morning beauty from her mortal day:
Down by the river of Adona her soft voice is heard;
And thus her gentle lamentation falls like morning dew.

O life of this our spring! Why fades the lotus of the water?
Why fade these children of the spring? Born but to smile &
fall.
Ah! Thel is like a watery bow, and like a parting cloud,
Like a reflection in a glass: like shadows in the water
Like dreams of infants, like a smile upon an infants face.
Like the doves voice, like transient day, like music in the air:
Ah! Gentle may I lay me down and gentle rest my head.
And gentle sleep the sleep of death, and gently hear the voice
Of him that walketh in the garden in the evening time.

The Lilly of the valley breathing in the humble grass
Answerd the lovely maid and said: I am a watery weed,
And I am very small and love to dwell in lowly vales:
So weak the gilded butterfly scarce perches on my head
Yet I am visited from heaven and he that smiles on all

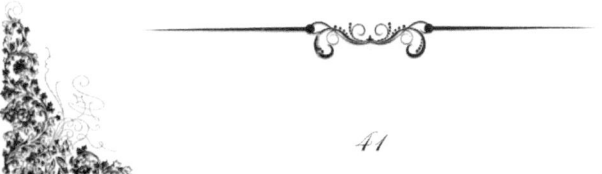

# Melpomene

Walks in the valley, and each morn over me spreads his hand
Saying, rejoice thou humble grass, thou new-born lily flower.
Thou gentle maid of silent valleys and of modest brooks:
For thou shall be clothed in light, and fed with morning manna:
Till summers heat melts thee beside the fountains and the springs
To flourish in eternal vales: they why should Thel complain.
Why should the mistress of the vales of Har, utter a sigh.

She ceased & smiled in tears, then sat down in her silver shrine.

Thel answered, O thou little virgin of the peaceful valley.
Giving to those that cannot crave, the voiceless, the o'er tired
The breath doth nourish the innocent lamb, he smells the milky garments
He crops thy flowers while thou sittest smiling in his face,
Wiping his mild and meeking mouth from all contagious taints.
Thy wine doth purify the golden honey; thy perfume.
Which thou dost scatter on every little blade of grass that springs
Revives the milked cow, & tames the fire-breathing steed.
But Thel is like a faint cloud kindled at the rising sun:
I vanish from my pearly throne, and who shall find my place.

Queen of the vales the Lily answered, ask the tender cloud,
And it shall tell thee why it glitters in the morning sky.
And why it scatters its bright beauty through the humid air.

## Melpomene

Descend O little cloud & hover before the eyes of Thel.

The Cloud descended and the Lily bowed her modest head:
And went to mind her numerous charge among the verdant grass.

II.

O little Cloud the virgin said, I charge thee to tell me
Why thou complainest now when in one hour thou fade away:
Then we shall seek thee but not find: ah Thel is like to thee.
I pass away, yet I complain, and no one hears my voice.

The Cloud then showed his golden head & his bright form emerg'd.
Hovering and glittering on the air before the face of Thel.

O virgin know'st thou not our steeds drink of the golden springs
Where Luvah doth renew his horses: lookst thou on my youth.
And fearest thou because I vanish and am seen no more.
Nothing remains; O maid I tell thee, when I pass away.
It is to tenfold life, to love, to peace, and raptures holy:
Unseen descending, weigh my light wings upon balmy flowers:
And court the fair eyed dew, to take me to her shining tent
The weeping virgin, trembling kneels before the risen sun.
Till we arise link'd in a golden band and never part:
But walk united bearing food to all our tender flowers.

*Melpomene*

Dost thou O little cloud?  I fear that I am not like thee:
For I walk through the vales of Har, and smell the sweetest flowers:
But I feed not the little flowers: I hear the warbling birds,
But I feed not the warbling birds, they fly and seek their food:
But Thel delights in these no more because I fade away
And all shall say, without a use this shining women lived,
Or did she only live to be at death the food of worms.

The Cloud reclind upon his airy throne and answered thus.

Then if thou art the food of worms, O virgin of the skies,
How great thy use, how great thy blessing, every thing that lives.
Lives not alone nor or itself: fear not and I will call,
The weak worm from its lowly bed, and thou shalt hear its voice.
Come forth worm and the silent valley, to thy pensive queen.

The helpless worm arose and sat upon the Lillys leaf,
And the bright Cloud saild on, to find his partner in the vale.


III.

Then Thel astonish'd view'd the Worm upon its dewy bed.

Art thou a Worm? Image of weakness, art thou but a Worm?
I see thee like an infant wrapped in the Lillys leaf;

# Melpomene

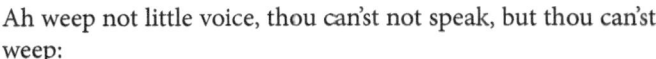

Ah weep not little voice, thou can'st not speak, but thou can'st weep:
Is this a Worm? I see they lay helpless & naked: weeping
And none to answer, none to cherish thee with mothers smiles.

The Clod of Clay heard the Worms voice & rais'd her pitying head:
She bowd over the weeping infant, and her life exhald
In milky fondness, then on Thel she fix'd her humble eyes;

O beauty of the vales of Har, we live not for ourselves,
Thou seest me the meanest thing, and so I am indeed:
My bosom of itself is cold, and of itself is dark,

But he that loves the lowly, pours his oil upon my head
And kisses me, and binds his nuptial bands around my breast.
And says; Thou mother of my children, I have loved thee
And I have given thee a crown that none can take away.
But how this is sweet maid, I know not, and I cannot know
I ponder, and I cannot ponder; yet I live and love.

The daughter of beauty wip'd her pitying tears with her white veil,
And said, Alas! I knew not this, and therefore did I weep:
That God would love a Worm I knew, and punish the evil foot
That wilful bruis'd its helpless form: but that he cherish'd it
With milk and oil I never knew, and therefore did I weep,
And I complaind in the mild air, because I fade away.
And lay me down in thy cold bed, and leave my shining lot.

Melpomene

Queen of the vales, the matron Clay answered: I heard thy
sighs.
And all thy moans flew o'er my roof, but I have call'd them
down:
Wilt thou O Queen enter my house, tis given thee to enter,
And to return: fear nothing, enter with thy virgin feet.


IV.


The eternal gates terrific porter lifted the northern bar:
Thel enter'd in & saw the secrets of the land unknown;
She saw the couches of the dead, & where the fibrous roots
Of every heart on earth infixes deep its restless twists:
A land of sorrows & of tears where never smile was seen.

She wandered in the land of clouds thro' valleys dark, listning
Dolors & lamentations: waiting oft beside the dewy grave
She stood in silence, listning to the voices of the ground,
Till to her own grave plot she came, & there she sat down.
And heard this voice of sorrow breathed from the hollow pit.

Why cannot the Ear be closed to its own destruction?
Or the glistening Eye to the poison of a smile!
Why are Eyelids stord with arrows ready drawn,
Where a thousand fighting men in ambush lie!
Or an Eye of gifts & graces showering fruits & coined gold!

# Melpomene

Why a Tongue impress'd with honey from every wind?
Why an Ear, a whirlpool fierce to draw creations in?
Why a Nostril wide inhaling terror trembling & affright
Why a tender curb upon the youthful burning boy?
Why a little curtain of flesh on the bed of our desire?

The Virgin started from her seat, & with a shriek,
Fled back unhindered till she came into the vales of Har.

# Liber

# Maeroris

# Melpomene

## Benediction

Charles Baudelaire

When by the changeless Power of a Supreme Decree
The poet issues forth upon this sorry sphere,
His mother, horrified, and full of blasphemy,
Uplifts her voice to God, who takes compassion on her.

"Ah, why did I not bear a serpent's nest entire,
Instead of bringing forth this hideous Child of Doom!
Oh cursèd be that transient night of vain desire
When I conceived my expiation in my womb!"

"Yet since among all women thou hast chosen me
To be the degradation of my jaded mate,
And since I cannot like a love-leaf wantonly
Consign this stunted monster to the glowing grate,"

"I'll cause thine overwhelming hatred to rebound
Upon the cursèd tool of thy most wicked spite.
Forsooth, the branches of this wretched tree I'll wound
And rob its pestilential blossoms of their might!"

So thus, she giveth vent unto her foaming ire,
And knowing not the changeless statutes of all times,
Herself, amid the flames of hell, prepares the pyre;
The consecrated penance of maternal crimes.

Yet 'neath th' invisible shelter of an Angel's wing

# Melpomene

This sunlight-loving infant disinherited,
Exhales from all he eats and drinks, and everything
The ever sweet ambrosia and the nectar red.

He trifles with the winds and with the clouds that glide,
About the way unto the Cross, he loves to sing,
The spirit on his pilgrimage; that faithful guide,
Oft weeps to see him joyful like a bird of Spring.

All those that he would cherish shrink from him with fear,
And some that waxen bold by his tranquility,
Endeavour hard some grievance from his heart to tear,
And make on him the trial of their ferocity.

Within the bread and wine outspread for his repast
To mingle dust and dirty spittle they essay,
And everything he touches, forth they slyly cast,
Or scourge themselves, if e'er their feet betrod his way.

His wife goes round proclaiming in the crowded quads—
"Since he can find my body beauteous to behold,
Why not perform the office of those ancient gods
And like unto them, redeck myself with shining gold?"

"I'll bathe myself with incense, spikenard and myrrh,
With genuflexions, delicate viandes and wine,
To see, in jest, if from a heart, that loves me dear,
I cannot filch away the hommages divine."

# Melpomene

"And when of these impious jokes at length I tire,
My frail but mighty hands, around his breast entwined,
With nails, like harpies' nails, shall cunningly conspire
The hidden path unto his feeble heart to find."

"And like a youngling bird that trembles in its nest,
I'll pluck his heart right out; within its own blood
drowned,
And finally to satiate my favourite beast,
I'll throw it with intense disdain upon the ground!"

Towards the Heavens where he sees the sacred grail
The poet calmly stretches forth his pious arms,
Whereon the lightenings from his lucid spirit veil
The sight of the infuriated mob that swarms.

"Oh blest be thou, Almighty who bestowest pain,
Like some divine redress for our infirmities,
And like the most refreshing and the purest rain,
To sanctify the strong, for saintly ecstasies."

"I know that for the poet thou wilt grant a chair,
Among the Sainted Legion and the Blissful ones,
That of the endless feast thou wilt accord his share
To him, of Virtues, Dominations and of Thrones."

"I know, that Sorrow is that nobleness alone,
Which never may corrupted be by hell nor curse,
I know, in order to enwreathe my mystic crown

# Melpomene

I must inspire the ages and the universe."

"And yet the buried jewels of Palmyra old,
The undiscovered metals and the pearly sea
Of gems, that unto me you show could never hold
Beside this diadem of blinding brilliancy."

"For it shall be engendered from the purest fire
Of rays primeval, from the holy hearth amassed,
Of which the eyes of Mortals, in their sheen entire,
Are but the tarnished mirrors, sad and overcast!"

# Melpomene

## Annabel Lee

Edgar Allan Poe

It was many and many a year ago,
In a kingdom by the sea,
That a maiden lived whom you may know
By the name of ANNABEL LEE;—
And this maiden she lived with no other thought
Than to love and be loved by me.

I was a child and She was a child,
In this kingdom by the sea,
But we loved with a love that was more than love—
I and my ANNABEL LEE—
With a love that the wingéd seraphs of Heaven
Coveted her and me.

And this was the reason that, long ago,
In this kingdom by the sea,
A wind blew out of a cloud by night
Chilling my ANNABEL LEE;
So that her high-born kinsmen came
And bore her away from me,
To shut her up, in a sepulchre
In this kingdom by the sea.

The angels, not half so happy in Heaven,
Went envying her and me:
Yes! that was the reason (as all men know,

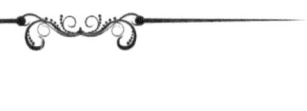

In this kingdom by the sea)
That the wind came out of the cloud, chilling
And killing my ANNABEL LEE.

But our love it was stronger by far than the love
Of those who were older than we—
Of many far wiser than we—
And neither the angels in Heaven above
Nor the demons down under the sea
Can ever dissever my soul from the soul
Of the beautiful ANNABEL LEE:—

For the moon never beams without bringing me dreams
Of the beautiful ANNABEL LEE;
And the stars never rise but I see the bright eyes
Of the beautiful ANNABEL LEE;
And so, all the night-tide, I lie down by the side
Of my darling, my darling, my life and my bride
In her sepulchre there by the sea—
In her tomb by the side of the sea.

# Melpomene

## The Dogs of War
## (While You Still Have A Voice)

*L. Alexander Carlé*

Cry havoc and let slip the dogs of war
Do nothing to stem the flow of blood
From veins to bloody floor
Your temperance be damned, you fool
You think that simple platitudes will save you?
The sword will brave your utterances and incantations
Speculations on how best to carve up thine wrists
Will spare you the rod of another man's hands
And throw light upon the thought ways
Of the creatures whose bones sit picked clean around you
Cry murder
Cry foul play
Just cry out the rivulets burning holes into your cheekbones
Slicing through ash and the program of fear
Written into your features
As you sit in sullen contemplation
Of how this might end for you
The flickers of fickle light exposing dirt under your finger-
nails
Cuticles pared back to bloody knuckles
Honeysuckles feeding from the filthy dripping faucet on
the corner
Brilliance turned to grey and muted brown
And down beneath the soldier's feet they fall

Their roots frozen into concrete as yours are
You shall not venture this way again
You shall not move from this moment
Where time stopped
And words failed

# Melpomene

## Lament

H. A. Cledones

No song, no dance - a hundred years of war have passed; the ballerina lies fallen, discarded hyacinths at her feet; the child of a ghost smiles - jackals pick the bones with Orpheus deceased, lost once more unto the maze - Persephone dethroned, the flowers wither; Eurydice returns to the grave cradling a serpents kiss - the venom burns, poisonous in ebony and emerald - the path downward spirals; Dante did not walk this passage - this is a dream of a seasons passing; born in a second - dead in a moment; reborn in fire - the blind dragon consumes it tail; the symphonic choir plays on; discord unheeded, Christ will not descend - the Harrowing does not come - barren of light, the leopard still prowls - only a tightrope spans the abyss - the maiden plays with lightening beneath the evening star; awaiting dawn - she plucks a swan for wings, catches butterflies between her teeth; spitting poppies from Lethe's kiss - its waters warm - drowning in memories with seaweed for hair; spring is forgotten and the ice will never thaw.

Cyclone - unfurl in tempestuous ardour for my thirteenth apostle of passion - I spilt the wine at supper; today it resembles blood, staining my virgins shroud - Judas kisses me again - judgement is at hand - I smell the unforeseen heavy in the air - my heart is to be weighed against a crows

feather, and the jury is blind - I want to throw away the rosemary and transform roses into lilies - innocence was my crime; ignorance is my plea - Let my carry my own coffin; I will rise again - three days dead for folly, awakened not by a prince but a leper - Poor Magdalene that I am - I misplaced a vision of crystal & gold; a year was lost to the storm winds; I forgot to sing with Sappho and delivered a flower of evil to Hell; the fairy-tale still did not come.

# Melpomene

## Deus erat Verbum

*Tamás Nagyatádi Horváth*

The most beatiful at the very heart
of the loneliness is the moment
when all of us are together
all of us who we were and who we are

we all who once just spoke to each other
whose eyes met once in the time
we who thought the same thoughts
from beyond and above different lights

all of us who once felt we share
the same lungs and the same heart
the same streams of blood in the same
blooming of different silences

so going here under for a while
where the slow blossom that is known
from the eternal summer of our kingdom
these petals are anyway just love

and even in this lack of magic
we can close our tired eyes diving
blinded the way as God loves us
in the infinite splendor of emanation

# Melpomene

## This Lost Shadow

*Ivor Steven*

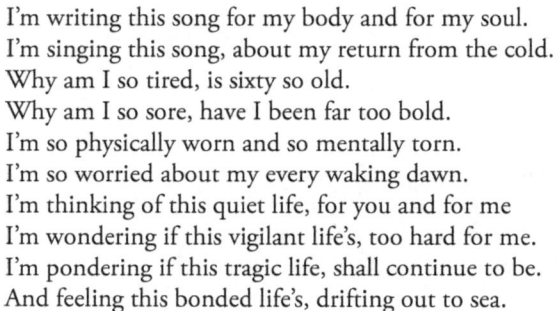

I'm writing this song for my body and for my soul.
I'm singing this song, about my return from the cold.
Why am I so tired, is sixty so old.
Why am I so sore, have I been far too bold.
I'm so physically worn and so mentally torn.
I'm so worried about my every waking dawn.
I'm thinking of this quiet life, for you and for me
I'm wondering if this vigilant life's, too hard for me.
I'm pondering if this tragic life, shall continue to be.
And feeling this bonded life's, drifting out to sea.

I'm writing these words for everyone to see.
I'm writing this book, about a single weeping tree.
Why am I so sleepy, am I aging too quickly.
Why am I so sad, who's looking after me.
I'm this furnace log, burning up with glee.
I'm this sinking boat, all about to flee.
I'm this overburdened camel, or a donkey maybe.
I'm this empty desert, a void, far as the eye can see.
I'm this broken branch, withering and dying, oh so slowly.
I'm this lost shadow, wandering this barren land furtively.

# Melpomene

## Sink Or Swim

Marg Howlett

You want to wallow in still waters
Like a whale that's drawn to shore
Or be like the spawning salmon
As it soars the waterfall
You want to hide amongst the corals
Or be camoflaged by reeds
As life has caused you havoc
Not what you had perceived
You want to dart,dash and flutter
From every shadow that you near
For the "jaws" of life to taunt you
So your addiction hides your fears
Or do you want to dance and play and chatter
Like the dolphins in the sea
To laugh and love and cherish
What life HAS given thee
The hook has held you often
You have felt it reel you in
You have fought but then forgotten
As the jagged hook went in
You can escape its clutches
To reclaim your life set free
Just pull or twist or struggle
To let yourself be free
To swim through life's adventures
Exploring what it brings

# Melpomene

The hooks the baits are warnings
So they will always touch your skin

# Melpomene

## Spleen

Paul Verlaine

The roses were so red, so red,
The ivies altogether black.

If you but merely turn your head,
Beloved, all my despairs come back!

The sky was over-sweet and blue,
Too melting green the sea did show.

I always fear, if you but knew!
From your dear hand some killing blow.

Weary am I of holly-tree
And shining box and waving grass

Upon the tame unending lea,
And all and all but you, alas!

Liber

Fatum

# Melpomene

## Ill Luck

Charles Baudelaire

This heavy burden to uplift,
O Sysiphus, thy pluck is required!
And even though the heart aspired,
Art is long and Time is swift.

Afar from sepulchres renowned,
To a graveyard, quite apart,
Like a broken drum, my heart,
Beats the funeral marches' sound.

Many a buried jewel sleeps
In the long-forgotten deeps,
Far from mattock and from sound;

Many a flower wafts aloft
Its perfumes, like a secret soft,
Within the solitudes, profound.

# Melpomene

## The Invisible Hand

James WF Roberts

Can you feel the world spinning now?
All around us?
Sitting in a car, on your way to work or school…
Like a top rotating on an uneven surface;
falling all over the place…

Lining up in a shop,
For the latest and greatest;
*"This is so much better than anything*
*That's ever gone before…"*

*Upgrade! Upgrade!*
*Manifest destiny;*
*Somehow sounds better than, the reality,*
*"This new product has all the features of the old one.*
*Upgrade! Upgrade! But it's the same thing,*
*with a new slim-lock design.*
*Mp3 USB drive for the car.*
*Blue tooth and GPS all you need for a night out on the town".*
*Upgrade! Upgrade!*

*Deep in outer space—*
*Our little blue rock, is covered by a malice,*
*That our kind has made for itself….*
*the invisible hand holds us all in place—*

*No matter where we are;*
*the selfless—become the selfish!*

Law-makers lie, every chance they get;
For our way of life to survive; they know deep down,
That the poor have to starve—so we can buy a car!

*Never think that's the kindness of the butcher,*
*The baker or the brewer, or even God, that we expect our dinner,*
*But from their regard to their own self interest.*

 *We address ourselves, not to their humanity*
   *But to their self-love.*
*Never talk to them of our own necessities but of their advantages*
*We are all just slaves to the invisible hand…*
*Not the hand of God;*
 *Nor the hand that spins the wheel of fate..*
*(Samsāra long gone now!)*

*No matter what the planet must run now,*
*Without government control!*
*Like a spinning top without control*
*Spinning now closer—closer towards the edge of the desk!*
*What happens when the Invisible hand starts to get Arthritic?*


*The Wealth of Nations; Adam Smith*

# Melpomene

## Red Aeon

Gwendolyn Taunton

Luminous scarlet bleeds
forlorn from the jagged wound of sundered sky.

The tongue of Mars flickers
a burning moth aflame from the ruptured celestial sanctuary

Heaven descends
a crimson Seraph wielding both glory and woe.

Destruction resplendent
singes the eyes of the immortal salamander casting forlorn
cinders adrift in snow.

Wormwood rises
bound by blood for the promise of an imperial dream.

Birthed and Swathed in carnage
steady hands reach to take the ruby from the Morning Stars
laurel of gold.

The Light itself is on fire
the Dark now burns and beginning and endings alike unfold.

# Melpomene

## Swimming in the Tear Drops of God.

James W.F. Roberts

the puppet is made not of material.
paper mache—wood nor paint.
      but clay.
skin. bone. blood. Soul!
a mind—not of one's own.

swimming in the tear drops of God.
  searching for a reason why.
why the world bleeds?
all the hurt, humanity breeds.
  why do we hurt?
      all the hatred we breed?

why we even born at all?

*swimming in the tear drops of God.*
like a puppet on a string,

I'm wrenched outta this sea of despair.
a girl with mirrored eyes
dances naked in the rain.
offers me an oaken chalice--
blood of Christ?

elixir of life?

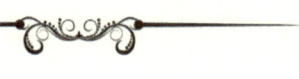

# *Melpomene*

in her eyes I see the world. as she
kisses my lips—

the stars turn cold. Earth stops. seasons fade.

like a child with a spinning top.
slowly moving in the other direction.
ancient pines and oak trees, descend to saplings—twigs.

swimming in the tear drops of God.
a butterfly whispers to me on the breeze.
Black soot invades nature's womb.

As we puncture mirror girl's stomach—from within.
the deeper we mine. the more ore and—more oil we require;
harder it is for her heart to pump blood—
to regulate her inner—our outer
temperature.

As love—imagination starts to dwindle.
and we pray to the fortress—

the prison of the mind; in our palms,
in the middle of the lounge—

on our laps, on our desks—at 2:15pm no new updates—
no missed calls. no spam. no infomercials;
has God deserted me?

you ask.

*does—*

# Melpomene

*can—*
      *has—*

*should God exist at all?*

# Melpomene

## The Sick Rose

William Blake

O rose, thou art sick!
The invisible worm,
That flies in the night,
In the howling storm,
Has found out thy bed
Of crimson joy,
And his dark secret love
Does thy life destroy.

# Melpomene

## Katabolé

Tamás Nagyatádi Horváth

As they were like silent ghosts only
on the black branches
even the birds did not yet learnt
their dew-dropping wake world songs

as nobody was yet heard even a shred
from the angel choir singing
the far sounding hymns of names
of the just created things and beings

as there were not divided
the streaming waters above
warm doom was arched across the skies
suffocated by oracular wants

whirling thoughts were stuck
one by one as incomprehensibly
and slowly started to change everything
shifting turning to irrevelance

finally as it was already readable
from the signs previously snow
started to fall and the landscape
changed into the shape of a hunted couple

# Melpomene

## Ashes

L. Alexander Carlé

What a brutal wreck of a man this is
The spiritual spawn of Midas' curse
But not to gold upon his touch
He leaves a trail of embers
Charred remains of tree trunks and friendly faces
Airs and graces fall to fears and frustrations
As he burns the ground around him
And sends the people scattering for cover
Friend and lover blackened by the brushstroke of fingertips
While food turns to ash upon his lips
Sulphur drifts to the toxic rivers at his feet
Running out in all directions
Laying waste to all they chance across
He has been here before
Seen these same sightless wrecks of men
No illusion of safety for them
Carbon clouds in air too thick to breathe
As he passes through this place
A wayfaring stranger
On his way to nowhere

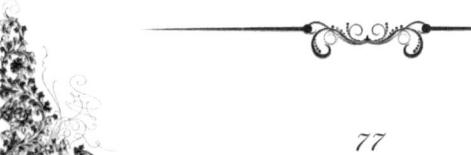

# Melpomene

## To Thee... Untitled

Bernardo Sena

Darkness inside, no where to look
Everything seems so distant, so far away
Come back another day and let me be
Do you know what could have been?
Keep away, and don't stare into the sun

I objectify the rejection of my own world
Through the lens of darkened reflection

If you look long enough you'll soon see a truth
Or a hidden reality we all fantasize for
The ultimate in virtual desire,
Propagation,
Annihilation,
Lo, behold the unanswered questions of dead thoughts
But no escape within the confines of delirium

Prisoners of what doom you make, this is your end

Final consumption, without demand...

# Melpomene

## Ghosts Before
## You're Dead

### Gene Banyard

I want to tell you about a time when it all went out, a time all too black. I do not know how it happened but I do know why it happened. You see, people are naturally lazy, not just as individuals but as a collective whole: everything always left until tomorrow, the last moment. Well "the last minute" came all right but it was far too late. The Rubicon thirst had been quenched. It had sucked dry all the dreams of a culture lost leaving their fancies and imaginings floundering on a polluted shore. The things they would create, the games they would play. Staring at screens and scribbling on walls. Distorting language, layering and cataloging realities, reading into the fiction instead of seeing the fact. Well, now we know the fact and they will never let us read again. Everything is now monitored and controlled. No thought or action ever steps out of line. They were just ghosts but they were ghosts before they were dead.

## Betrayed With a Kiss

James WF Roberts

With heaven on their minds,
They made me damned for all of time,
Me, just the puppet on a string,
Dangling on every breath, every word…
Not such a man of wealth and taste,

To-morrow, and to-morrow, and to-morrow,
Creeps in this petty pace from day to day,
To the last syllable of recorded time;

And all our yesterdays have lighted fools
So, soon the pages of antiquity, turn against
Those who were doing, what they were told,

The plague of humanity, condemns, oh so quickly
The false-acting man, all the world knows,
*Don't they,* my Dice was loaded?
The odds stacked up way too high?

The 2,000 year poster child
For the wicked, the cruel and the wild
Condemned for a crime,
I had no choice but to commit

Thirty shiny silver coins, led us to this place, now!

# Melpomene

In a festive garden, olives, wine

The bitterness *of that* kiss
Of a brother, who died at the hands,
Of his own kind!

I had no choice,
The Righteous and the brave,
Led me away, telling me,
Not to let the mob lead us astray

The echoes of time,
The shadows of pain,
Led me time and time again,
To pray for anything to happen, but what did!
Now lost in a dismal haze,

As I now gathered up the bloodied coins,
Tossing them into a dried river bed,
My shame, my sorrow,
My forgiveness, salvation,
A noose around a tree…
The most revered and celebrated,
Betrayed our brother,
At the crack of dawn, three times
Yet, I followed what the old visions said….

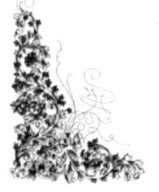

# Melpomene

## Sentience

Gene Banyard

Alone in a deserted alleyway, perched on a skip like a starving bird. Fingers worn by weathered nights of clawing misery which we pray, somehow, to forget, let alone forgive. Within the concrete void a cast iron fist is raised to the blackened sky.

Petals of blade and malice slew miserating flesh in a gradient of life and the never born as carnality collapses beneath grates of metal in a cold and sharp universe.

Blood in the gutter and closure in the bones.

Liber

Mortuorum

# Melpomene

## The Death of the Lovers

Charles Baudelaire

We will have beds which exhale odours soft,
We will have divans profound as the tomb,
And delicate plants on the ledges aloft,
Which under the bluest of skies for us bloom.

Exhausting our hearts to their last desires,
They both shall be like unto two glowing coals,
Reflecting the twofold light of their fires
Across the twin mirrors of our two souls.

One evening of mystical azure skies,
We'll exchange but one single lightning flash,
Just like a long sob—replete with good byes.

And later an angel shall joyously pass
Through the half-open doors, to replenish and wash
The torches expired, and the tarnished glass.

# Melpomene

## Colloque Sentimental

Paul Verlaine

In the deserted park, silent and vast,
Erewhile two shadowy glimmering figures passed.

Their lips were colorless, and dead their eyes;
Their words were scarce more audible than sighs.

In the deserted park, silent and vast,
Two spectres conjured up the buried past.

"Our ancient ecstasy, do you recall?"
"Why, pray, should I remember it at all?"

"Does still your heart at mention of me glow?
Do still you see my soul in slumber?" "No!"

"Ah, blessed, blissful days when our lips met!
You loved me so!" "Quite likely, - I forget."

"How sweet was hope, the sky how blue and fair!"
"The sky grew black, the hope became despair."

Thus walked they 'mid the frozen weeds, these dead,
And Night alone o'erheard the things they said.

# Melpomene

## The Conqueror Worm

Edgar Allan Poe

LO! 'Tis a gala night
Within the lonesome latter years!
An angel throng, bewinged, bedight
In veils, and drowned in tears,
Sit in a theatre, to see
A play of hopes and fears,
While the orchestra breathes fitfully
The music of the spheres.

Mimes, in the form of God on high,
Mutter and mumble low,
And hither and thither fly—
Mere puppets they, who come and go
At bidding of vast formless things
That shift the scenery to and fro,
Flapping from out their Condor wings
Invisible Woe!

That motley drama—oh, be sure
It shall not be forgot!
With its Phantom chased for evermore,
By a crowd that seize it not,
Through a circle that ever returneth in
To the self-same spot,
And much of Madness, and more of Sin,
And Horror the soul of the plot.

# Melpomene

But see, amid the mimic rout
A crawling shape intrude!
A blood-red thing that writhes from out
The scenic solitude!
It writhes!—it writhes!—with mortal pangs
The mimes become its food,
And the angels sob at vermin fangs
In human gore imbued.

Out—out are the lights—out all!
And, over each quivering form,
The curtain, a funeral pall,
Comes down with the rush of a storm,
And the angels, all pallid and wan,
Uprising, unveiling, affirm
That the play is the tragedy, "Man,"
And its hero the Conqueror Worm.

# Melpomene

## The Chariot

*Emily Dickinson*

Because I could not stop for Death,
He kindly stopped for me;
The carriage held but just ourselves
And Immortality.

We slowly drove, he knew no haste,
And I had put away
My labor, and my leisure too,
For his civility.

We passed the school where children played,
Their lessons scarcely done;
We passed the fields of gazing grain,
We passed the setting sun.

We paused before a house that seemed
A swelling of the ground;
The roof was scarcely visible,
The cornice but a mound.

Since then 't is centuries; but each
Feels shorter than the day
I first surmised the horses' heads
Were toward eternity.

# Melpomene

## A Poison Tree

*William Blake*

I was angry with my friend:
I told my wrath, my wrath did end.
I was angry with my foe:
I told it not, my wrath did grow.
And I watered it in fears
Night and morning with my tears,
And I sunned it with smiles
And with soft deceitful wiles.

And it grew both day and night,
Till it bore an apple bright,
And my foe beheld it shine,
And he knew that it was mine,—

And into my garden stole
When the night had veiled the pole;
In the morning, glad, I see
My foe outstretched beneath the tree.

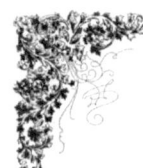

# Melpomene

## Tenderness of God

Azsacra Zarathustra

*Dedicated to Dr. Santosh Kumar*

### SURVIVAL — DENIES — PRESERVATION

URKH 1

It's Cruel Snow
But Not The Sun
That Fondles Feathers Of The Bird —
The She-Wolf — Led By The Fire That Burns —
Madly Quickens  Her Run

It's Only Possible To Die
Without Cry But Full Of Fower —
Small Copper Change Is Hid And Covered
By Scattered Diamonds

It's Only Possible To Kill
The Reason Of Being And Of Aim —
He Who Will Shoot Himself In Head
Of Thrill Will Tear The Thread

## Melpomene

URKH 2

Half-Open Are The Eyes Of Blaze
But Rage Of Day Does Not Abate —
The Hawk Of Vengeance Flies Away
To Count The Righteous
And Replete

The Unity Of Owls And The Moon —
The Eyes See Light In Their Blindness —
And Slowly Is Reduced To Ashes By The Fire
The Eagles' Blood

For Kiss There Is — A Bite And Death —
To Feel The Pain The Birds Will Fly —
And Wolves — The Killers That Are Wise —
Will Force —
The Weak —
To Die


URKH 3

Fall Asleep — At The End Of The Day —
The Moon Turns The Way Into Ashes —
In The Ominous Play Of The Flame
There Is Nothing But God's Tenderness

There Is Nothing But Reinforced Purity —

# Melpomene

What Love Forbids Is Defied —
It Is Darkness In Its Fury
That Saves
The Light

It Is The Wisdom Of The Slayer
That Strives The Living To Unravel —
He Who Tomorrow The Truth Will Reveal
Is Bound To Die — Today


URKH 4

Death
Creating The Beauty
Will Always Overcome —
And What Is Really Red Like Blood —
Will Shine
And Shimmer Bright

What's Really — Really Black —
Will Keep The Thrill Inside —
Every Innocent Hides
The Evil And Rebellious

It's Tenderness That Calls
To Torture And Demolish —
The Flight Of Deathly Claws —
Will Make — The Pure —

Flourish

URKH 5

So Frozen In The Deathlike Fire
The Birds Are Silently Flying —
And In The Center Of Outlined Range
Still Furious —
They —
Alight

The Whirlwind Of The Snow Again
Makes Deathly Purity Attractive —
You Are — Whose Truth Is — Nowhere
You Are — Whose Sense Is —
To Attack

You'll Have The Sun All To Yourselves —
But Shadows Of The Moon Fly High —
And Claws So Tenderly Will Touch
My Lips

URKH 6

Him Who Has Unleashed The War
Killing Never Pangs —
All Money's To The Flare Thrown

To Let The Fire Reign

And Females Are Given To Males
To Feel The Joy Of Copulation —
For Beauty And For Revelation
A Temple From Skulls
Is Made

Let The White Sheets Burn Away —
No Steps Do The Flying Want —
Into The Space Of New Void
Shadows Are Cast
By The Wing


URKH 7

The Harmony And Blood Are Bound —
You Eagles Live To Hunt —
The Arrow Is Touched By The Palm —
And Freezes
The Feverish Body

The Blade Is Touched By The Palm
To Make The Revelation Bright —
And Birds Of Predatory Psalms
Fly High — And Cry

The War Is Always Summing Up —

For Love There's No Perfection —
Let Us Forget The Heavenly Attractions
THE CRUELTY IS
TENDERNESS
OF GOD

# Melpomene

## Real

*Emily Dickinson*

I like a look of agony,
Because I know it's true;
Men do not sham convulsion,
Nor simulate a throe.

The eyes glaze once, and that is death.
Impossible to feign
The beads upon the forehead
By homely anguish strung.

# Melpomene

## The Corpse

C. B. Liddell

The Corpse looked at me from the place where he died
I said, 'The World's moved on since then
I don't know how many miles'

*"But I died where you lie,"* he said
*"I died right by your side*
*and if you look around you'll see some others just like me'*

And truth enough
in the shadows of the room I saw
other faces glowing white, shadowy eyes, and quivering lips
as if some tale to tell
They all said the same old thing
*"We died here as well"*

*"I was in the forest when I broke my leg and died"*
Another opened wide his mouth
His tale was just a cry
but I saw the spear come through
and burst his bulging eye

*"I was sacrificed to God*

# Melpomene

*They built a shrine for me*
*And where you lie, they raised me high*
*and plunged a knife in me"*

Another with a gentler face had a softer tale to tell:
*"I was old, it was cold: my journey's end was near*
*I made a fire over here, and let the fire die*
*Drinking mead, I went to sleep, the sweetest sleep there is"*

Another with a hungry face
hovered over me
*"Here it was I had my home. I built a little hut*
*and killed my lord's wild game when there*
*was nothing else to eat*
*And for my crime he hung me high*
*Right by my gate I died"*

All night the spirits talked to me
How crowded was their world
*"In every place you go,"* they said
*"Someone must there have died"*

I asked them why they told me this
They laughed and said, *"You'll know –*

# Melpomene

*this morning when they come to wake*
*your cold and lifeless corpse"*

# Melpomene

## The Residual Decline

Bernardo Sena

I walk the lonely path of my own dementia
Like some nomadic shaman on his path
With nowhere to go and nothing to recognise
I am all alone in my world of ordered chaos
No meaning in this fragmented dream

I have been told everything all my life
That which I can never have
I can't even make sense of words
I can't even make sense of thoughts
When will I free myself from all or nothing?

Trapped in a complex labyrinth of madness
No escape from the reality surrounding me
Catching up to my purposeless existence
Death is too easy, only self-inflicted pity
No control over your choice in destiny

Free will is the lie told to us when we're young
Born into a senseless, logical world
Trapped by our very own primal desires
Nowhere tomorrow, gone yesterday

I will not cry, or lash out... I must try harder

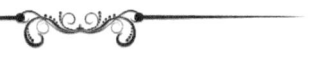

*Melpomene*

I have been told everything all my life
That which I have always dreamed of
I can't even make sense of others
I can't even make sense of my Self
When may I sleep the endless slumber?

My feelings have long since died
The emotions are all but drained
No longer can I continue
The charade that plays in my head
Long live remorseless insanity

I look into my reflection in the mirror
I am disappearing piece by piece...
That man is no longer who I am
But something which I never was
I am that I am...

# Melpomene

## The Dance of Kali

Gwendolyn Taunton

Time fades in the passage of morning, slumbering peacefully upon the shallow graves of still-born hours. Sepulchers of the departed lie unnamed like specters basking in an ethereal light with limbs of granite extended skywards to an unknown god who hides away his fifth and final head. Truth reaches beyond the embrace of Death and her Fair Twin who lay coiled together like serpents, forever entwined in dreamless sleep. And when they waken? The endless moment when immortality is realised and the centuries pass as mere seconds. The bite of an apple. The cry of a child. The withering of flesh. The experience of eternity in the fluttering of an eyelid and the dream that sets alight butterfly wings…

Life billows as sand in the winds down the corridor of the infinite; dust in the eyes of divinity - erasing the emptiness from all history with a casual and relentless gesture that belies contempt for our monuments, branding us as nothing more than a hairless ape that reaches vainly for the fruits of knowledge - the imperfect creation of an imperfect God. The mirror shatters, and the banshee screams.

*Is this life or just an echo of life?* The definitions of reality and epistemology elude, confuse and confound the finite. It is a conundrum for the wise and a riddle for the brave.

# Melpomene

The scions of the fallen perish inside the conjectures and parables of those who have sought this path before. The meaning has become entangled in too many words, speculation and hyperbole. The propaganda of those immersed in idolatry offers nothing but fatigue - and after this exegesis; what then is left to ponder? *A riddle; perchance a single rhyme? A thinly disguised icon standing aghast at the doors of ruin. The deepest secrets are buried deep beyond word, wrapped in nous and logos. The veil can be lifted from the holiest of mysteries only by the hands of the blind, and grail grasped by deed alone. No word can be uttered to break the silence of the endless moment and the sensation which stands beyond expression. In solitude alone will Truth lift her veil.*

The secret is buried deep in the attic of the soul; withered like autumn, cracked like glass. Herein, atop the surface, the monsters dwell, prowling like demons in the dark. Changing and reflecting paradigms, algorithms and the purest essence of the terror which cannot reason. The spiral staircase to the upper regions of the subconscious, lies shrouded in blackest shades, obscuring the evil none can see. In fear of Fear, there is nothing save the hissing of beasts within.

*Wherefore now then?* Everywhere save this route has been chartered, except this forbidden highway to the palace of wisdom. There is no road which has not been traversed, no

# Melpomene

river yet to forge. Only crossroads loom, their ragged signs extended overhead, gazing downwards. Which sign should be heeded, which chapter revisited - *The Past? Present? Or Future? The maiden lifts her veil, to reveal the last illusion.*

I see the great basilisk swallow its tail; by doing so it devours time also. The great serpent paralyses, poisons the blood with the venom and language of birds.

The spiral encloses itself in the fractal of chaos; it is both the labyrinth and the twine which guides the explorer towards the center. There are no more roads, only the vague outline of footsteps, a trail that has gone unseen. Ignoring the beasts, they crawl towards the centrifuge, their voices and thoughts a cacophony of dread and dreams for those who have learned to hear beyond sound and look beyond sight.

*Thou shalt not? Or Thou will not? Oedipus lies dead at the feet of the manticore.*

This knowledge is like a stone; the strong shall bear it aloft with both shoulders, but sometimes the boulder slips; cracking fragile bones, cleaving the flesh in two. And if this burden were dropped, who would listen? The ears are swollen shut, blocked by the echo of Narcissus's whispers. *Does wisdom set boundaries even to knowledge?* Such distractions are unbecoming to art – divinity is not for bliss; pleasure is not for salvation. Within the eyes of Truth

– both Beauty and Infinity. Rotten, the apple falls from the ground shattering the solace of Eden and humanity is left to cradle the corpse of the Ideal with tentative jealousy; Truth alone possesses the hymns of Orpheus, chanted from deep within the gates of horn and ivory. Guarded by chimeras and salamanders, Three Sisters sing weaving Beauty from flesh and bone, hiding murmured secrets in the peripheral visions of a world yet to come.

The Graces descend, their virtues now transcend as flaws, weapons of elegance which have been deployed to destroy. The Ideal pursued unto its bitter end becomes a crucifix, the crux of innocence upon which to be impaled, arms outstretched, opened wide... the gravity of ascension sometimes breaks the wings.

*I have fallen down from my perch atop the cross, onto the skulls and bones which line the ruins of Golgotha...I crawl amidst the mud, amongst the worms which gnaw sharply at my heart...Begrimed by the sustenance of the world, completed by the obscuration of form, the singing soil stings eyes. I rule absolute in the filth; a Demiurge of Dirt, Decay and Disease...from the heart of Time I craft a prison of bones and design a new Ideal. I baptize my carrion eagle with the wings of the Erinyes, glistening like Erebos, as beautiful as Nyx...not the last, but the first Prophet of the Abyss - the blade, the wound, the priest and the heretic, completed and forged by the Absence of Being, my Avatar encircles the*

# Melpomene

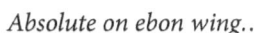

*Absolute on ebon wing...*

This perfect Muse can destroy, she is the beauty which slays; intoxicated with destruction, her half murmured promises strike like blades, which she whispers in tones of velvet and honey. She wields a singular rose for cruelty, the gift of thorns, and for her most beloved, Wormwood mixed with Seraphim tongue.

The black soil sings once more. Its aria begins with but a single blade of grass. The masquerade of Truth marches ever onwards to her rhythms of war. Carcass upon carcass; the insects devour and despair – innocence has always been their feast. *Eat to live....Kill to live...*Where in life is the compensation for reoccurrence? It is not the eyes of mercy which stare into our recesses -The kiss of this Lady always tastes of musk and the grave. Her whispers freeze the air with every half-murmured word;

*"Wherefore now my Silent One? Why elude the image of my piety? Silence is ever the bearer of sterility. Taste in my stillness - let my tranquility illuminate your dream lit world. I am the eidolon of Truth itself - when I cease only emptiness is found."*

Here in exile from the womb, in the shell of flesh in another fraction of time and space, in dissolution we are born content, dwelling in the fragments, where reason breaks down and from is absolved. Clothed in sky and aether we

reel; the horror of comprehension is the first realization of life.

*The separateness - the awareness of identity. To be torn away from totality and cast into loneliness.* How to rationalize the gulf between what was, what is and what is now becoming? Even the use of the pronouns becomes unprecedented - how can one be but a singular identity when nothing remains but abstraction? The material world constricts the passageways of communication - the very nature of the organic censures thought and impediments speech. The physical entrapment results in sorrow; it is *skin and bones which have embittered us.* Imprisoned in a cage of flesh, already preparing for another funeral when we ought to rejoice. At best, random catalysts that are reborn from age to age, in the passing of dust and decline.

*A reason perhaps?* Then deep it has been hidden behind this facade of Truth. There is neither a how nor a why. And although none know how to possess a way, my kin shall pass you by, for devoid of haste, you stumble, unaware that having beheld Truth we have learnt to envy ignorance...

*The Hourglass is ever poised to shatter.* I would murmur a warning but I cannot be heard amidst the idle chatter of a thousand rattling tongues for which I see no faces, only the voices of strangers - I know them better than they know themselves - this moment was created a lifetime ago; it was reborn only when the moon engulfed the sun.

# Melpomene

The boundaries between worlds are as thin as the silk of lotus petals, dreams are the fragrant flowers on which they alight; in sleep visions manifest – the distinctions between ecstasy and nightmare shatter in the bliss of midnight. I hear the clock chime thirteen - unlucky for some, but the laws of action have never bore me ill. The sensations are numbing; in hallucinations I see a serpent arise from the flaming jaws of a phoenix, scarlet and ivory intermingled but never mixing to the shade of rose.

Prophecy is my art - I have blinded my eyes with a jewel encrusted diadem of thorns, transformed my riddles into words; but my rhythm remains unknown. Delusion is the only illusion I have chosen to weave in strands of winding blades which contort, scarred by the light of hollow silver...

I circle my web all the more tighter, in and out the maze with the twine, borrowing the eye of a harpy crone in a mantle of stained sterling gray so that I may once more see. - She chants to me the hymn of Lilith yet does not remove her feathers. Her advice for me?

*'To Hades art thou wed daughter of spring. In winter alone shall you ever be content. You shall be the adjudicator of longing, the judge of lust and the conspirator of failure, your name will be reviled in every language and praised in every nation.'"*

# Melpomene

Why not take refuge in madness? Just to taste the merciful release but once - I yearn for that moment in which I could take repose from myself and look upon the world through the gaze of an absent stranger who views eternity from a dispossessed window. For this blissful turning, this enduring transmission of the eons flow, I would then cease and loose the shades within. How the mad must revel in their intoxicated freedom…Dionysus what a Lord thou art, wielding pleasure in one hand and torment in the other, what would you bestow upon me with thy satyrs kiss? Grapes of Wrath? Should the whispers of my psyche fail to please thy gilded ears will your fair entourage rend my body askew and my head away, holding it decapitated and bloody, to audience who weeps tears that are not born of woe…?

It is all lies - tales to scare children from their slumber; I have died again. *The resurrection has begun. The sins of the past fall away like autumn leaves.* I hold their withered skins to my own; we are the parchment of eternity, the World Tree and I. The leaves crumble at my touch, blowing away in the gale, adrift on the billowing winds of infinity. *The night is black, formless and cold. Winter approaches again.*

Compared to my heart, the ice is warm, for I have been shunned - driven away like an animal lest my basilisk's stare freezes the cattle to death. Homeless, I have returned here, to the chambers of sorrow, where the baleful eyes of the lost ones beg intrepidly for the sun; for spring to thaw

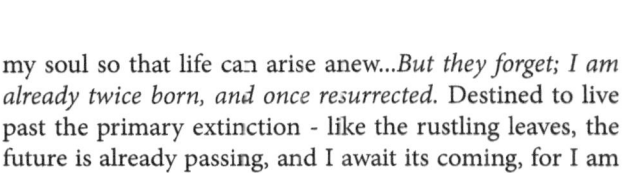

my soul so that life can arise anew...*But they forget; I am already twice born, and once resurrected.* Destined to live past the primary extinction - like the rustling leaves, the future is already passing, and I await its coming, for I am saddened by communication with the damned.

But, where are the ghouls, the ones who will consume the decay? *Has their appetite already been satiated?* Need I no longer shed my blood for ink - there are still many ripe verses inside my veins, my devils quill still drips fresh upon my parchment of virginal skin. Maybe I should now scribe my desires with a syringe to inject my venom? *There is no antidote I can prescribe for such substantial redemption.* It is only the ghosts who linger on to listen. The scavengers will progress onwards to a carcass with more meat - real predators are always in search of an easier meal. My blood in nothing new to these aristocrats of the hunt, even though I have bathed entire fields of lilies in red...

*The waters alone will melt the frost.* Only then will the Sun have driven the snows away and return the cycle to spring. Fertile seeds probing in the ground tendrils arise. *A thaw already?* My breath is like fog in the morning - a misty haze across the dew. Beginnings and endings are always quiet; repose gives birth to vigour. Wind strikes the moors so barren, lashes at my hair. The light is soft and for once my eyes reflect its radiance, though the glow is still all too faint - I can only burn in darkness, in daylight you will see neither my horns nor my halo. I have surrendered Lucifer's

crown, plucked out the single emerald eye and returned it to the Grail, once torn from the arms of a reluctant saint and thrice blessed by the king of fools.

Around me the animals dance to and fro, enacting the elaborate patterns of evolution, competing for the right to survive. Lex Talonis. Nature does not embody mercy. My favorite children in this garden are those who learnt to survive by tooth and claw. *Predator or prey: Which am I? At what point does one become the other?*

The grass is rusting - summer looms and the heat is visible. I can smell the turning of the seasons. Sluggish, fat with nourishment, life is at its peak. Even birds and fish slow down to rest before Truth again approaches. Basking in comfort, this is almost the standstill I have sought, but this repose does not engender contemplation. The desert may bring me more; for there is knowledge in the extremities, its harshness may bring me strength. A crimson soaked orb hovers relentlessly above, pouring its heat upon me with scorn, burning and searing my skin with savagery. It offers no compassion, not to I who am both pariah and wanderer. This is the time of cruelty, the severity of summer. Flies cling to me; swarm around my mouth and seek to fill my mouth with maggots - imperiously I wave them away, but there are too many - out of weariness I surrender my flesh to vermin, letting them crawl across my skin and vomit on my flesh...

# Melpomene

Food is scarce here; the young and the weak have already fallen. Jackals pick away at their bones, stripping clear the meat from the haunches of abandoned children. The bones of the unburied dead are all around me, festering as open sores on the surface of the earth. The ghostly laugh of the hyenas echoes in the heat drenched air. Raucously they howl, spurred on by the carnage wrought in the seasons change.

I feel ill - there is disease in my veins, nausea in my throat - I burn with lust and fever - the heat colors my thoughts with rage. It is only now that I am possessed by delirium that finally Beauty appears - the world dissolves away before me and I collapse to the ground, wilting, withering like a flower, spiraling down into the litter of bones and human remains...Dying, I leave my eyes wide open, transfixed to watch this phantom ballet unfurl before me, and to look with wonder towards sights previously unseen...

Twin cobras coil around me, as dark and as smooth as obsidian, sliding gently across my limbs, folding me in their reptilian embrace. They twist around me and rise above my head, stretching their proud, hooded heads atop my own, extending mouths and fangs with a rhythmic hiss - the serpents seek to shelter me from the Sun - whilst they possess life I still exist.

*Why now do I fear? Is this not the end for which I had hoped? Death hides behind her last illusion, Truth remains veiled.*

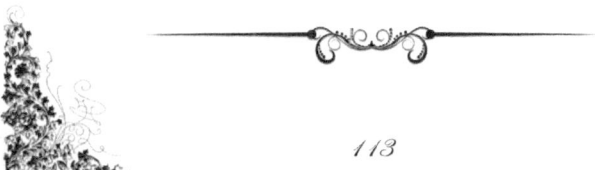

# Melpomene

I try to rise, I try to will - but I am spellbound by the grace of my visions...I hear operas composed by gilded flames, I see nymphs feasting in Sylvan glades, I inhale the scent of a thousand orchids, I taste nectars born of Gods and feel the softest caress of silk glide across my skin....*Illusions are by their nature sweet and this is the sign by which to know them.* That my dreams be so blissful - it is a sign that Beauty surely comes. Powerless, I can do nothing but watch the hapless theatre of my own psyche conjure phantasmagoria.

*What comes first?* The ghost of childhood lost. She smells of faded sunlight, nostalgia, and a desperate longing for remembrance. Her smile is pure, innocent, beguiling. Her eyes dance with amber and violet, dawn and dusk exist in harmony within - no good, no evil, no burdens of knowledge, no trials of experience. *My heart breaks when I look at her, when I look at what I might have been.*

*She picks irises and rosemary from the gardens of my pain, Laughs with all the delights of spring. She fears neither the summer nor the winter - She knows no terror of heat or cold. Delight alone has this woman-child seen.*

Unscarred by cruelty, bereft of the wisdom that it brings, She dances around the rose trees, laying a trail of blossoms behind her. Fairies fly about her bright and shining face, toying with the gloss of her platinum hair, Weaving laurels of gold and oak for my specters pretty head.

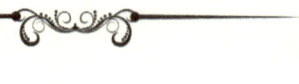

# Melpomene

*My tears fall upon the petals that she wantonly discards, for each one represents a sin. I wish that I could be this child of innocence again, to renounce all my self-imposed laments. I would do anything to raise this child of mine from back amongst the dead, Breathing life into her tender image - but she will never smile again. I know this because it was I myself who killed her.*

*And now?* Elusive hope. For once the taste of life sits still upon my tongue. I feel the fleeting pleasure of contentment near my tarnished soul. Angel's wings brush the apex of my heart, a pristine wake of feathers to cascade like kaleidoscopic waterfalls, into the core of my tattered being. *Could this indeed be the Ideal Moment? That dream which I have doggedly pursued unto my own bitter end?*

*The Sun also rises* - I have never before beheld the dawn, nor the colors of the incandescent sky dancing in the play of morning - by these signs I know your presence. Surely at last you are here. Contented, I find myself growing weary of words. Be silent now - *grant me peace - no more riddles - no more banquets with wolves.*

And there, reflected in a single second, the memories of dust, death and the taste of the grave. There I dwell in silence amidst the ruins of former opulence; at one with my surroundings, for we have both fallen to entropy. Exhausted and fatigued, the will to life has been surpassed.

Inside the room, once so exquisite, has begun to rot - insects gnaw at the fabrics of the windows heart, beneath the gaping wounds left by creature's jaws; nothing - the furniture itself seems to disappear.

The wine I sip from a fractured goblet has long since turned sour, but I pay no heed to its rancid flavour - like all true artists I have learned to appreciate the sting of acid.

The decor here was once scarlet shot with a twist of vermilion and splendid gold - it is now all faded to enduring brown; the shade of excrement. I used to love this room where I would once tap delightful tunes, but now it is discordant, broken, it plays only the melodies of Hell.

I cannot leave this place; memories hold me in bondage to the past - imprisoned by nostalgia, I can find no words for fond farewells.

The future abandoned, I find happiness only in ages past -memories of a persistent kiss linger on my lips, waltzing while the rain pours steadily to the strains of a delicate symphony - all dust. My world *-my domain has ended here* - I am too afraid to journey upwards.

Beyond the room a staircase ascends, winding upwards, there are monstrosities circling the shadows, in the darkness and the unknown...I cannot walk it for fear that terror makes its abode upstairs. Sometimes I dare to face

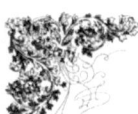

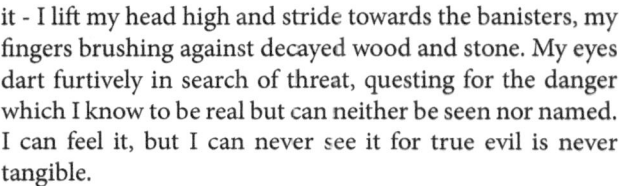

it - I lift my head high and stride towards the banisters, my fingers brushing against decayed wood and stone. My eyes dart furtively in search of threat, questing for the danger which I know to be real but can neither be seen nor named. I can feel it, but I can never see it for true evil is never tangible.

Bravely, I set my foot upon the first of many stairs, and the world proceeds to fall away...solidarity vanishes beneath my feet. The ground itself is devoured, and the walls are swallowed by a terrible all consuming darkness hungering to fill its void with the warmth of the living; all that is left now is the staircase, extending upwards like the Tower of Babel to the heart of the Abyss itself.

*There can be no turning back now.* I cling to it, to the crutch of my fear, least I plummet into the nothingness which yawns below snapping at my heels, there is no route now but upwards; the journey begun there is nothing but the route to ascension. Around me the void howls its displeasure; my frail body is assaulted by the winds of storm and fury - the unseen kisses and strokes the nape of my neck with icy talons, hissing into my ears, reaching and tightening its grip around my quivering throat...

One last effort - I evade these horrors which exist beyond form, falling gasping to the landing atop the stairs - a door bars my way and I feel the beasts behind me snatching at my Achilles heel; drawing blood that glistens as tiny red

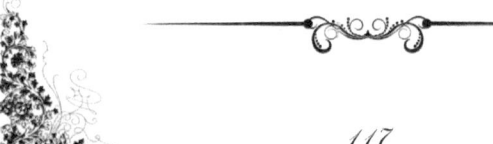

suns in the echoing darkness. I reach for the brass handle which is before me - fresh and new -it shines like hope - warm and comforting.

The door opens; the ghosts melt into the night which first gave them birth. I sigh with relief for the sight that greets me is a familiar one. I wipe away my blood and tears and enter my room of discolored reds. Seating myself once more upon the worn couch, I taken the broken goblet in my hand, drinking again the sour yet cherished wine of my memories - my ordeal never to forget - thankful that I have survived but never questioning.

*Drinking deep of Lethe and oblivion, already I forget the staircase, for I would prefer to remember only the room.*

Another life is gone. Once again I am returned to purgatory, on the journey to the iron city with the burning center – wherein spirals themselves do degrade, the ghost bride dogs at my heels as trinity bleeds a tear; my double headed jackal turns – uttering consummate belief in tongues unspoken – Coptic codes which cannot be deciphered; I had thought the voyage passed but the ship of the damned lays harbored still – in shadowed waters silhouetted by the shadows of beasts unknown – krakens which do not sleep and haunt the oceans of the mind...

*My double, my own soul, we still circle our prey in harmony,*

# *Melpomene*

*down in the depths...fragment, why will you remain my scion, and not yet meld?* Broken and discarded, my decadent melodies have lost the charms of revelry - the notes of joy are long forgotten...

I descend into the waters of memory, basking amongst the creatures of the deep and let tranquility wash over me – eyes dancing with ocean lights - I lay passive with the unseen, awaiting my final virtue; awaiting the embrace of the fathoms where Leviathan, my truth, can swallow me whole. Only immersion in the waters can cease my endless doctrine of burning.

As fluid I shall bow, malleable to eternity; *the waters of time shape all that is - stone and steel erode beneath ebbing flow.* Shape me waters, bestow form on that which dimension eludes, for as mist I cannot be...quell my flames. I care not where your current drifts; the tide shall always bear me home. Overtime, the steady currents erode even the hardest rock.

*I am destined to lose the struggle but to win the war. Only the strongest willow learns to bend. The fluid nature of power has no shape; all that remains is for the waters to run their course and devour the serpent. The liquidity of Time is the last illusion of Beauty, and Truth is the mask of Time. This is the riddle that only Death can understand.*

\*\*\*

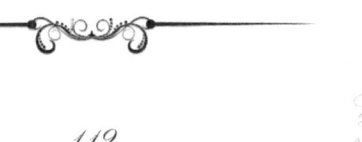

# Melpomene

"I am terrible Time the destroyer of all beings in all worlds, engaged to destroy all beings in this world; of those heroic soldiers presently situated in the opposing army, even without you none will will be spared."

*- Bhagavad Gita, 11:32*

# Melpomene

## Cold

Gene Banyard

A cemetery pauses in an autumnal forest where the tears of a thousand cats create dew in the absence of leaves. A small boy of no particular design or fancy listens to the click-a-clack of automata configured by clockwork match men. Walls crack and the worm bleeds.

I am cold.

# Melpomene

## Ashes Hollow

Christopher Pankhurst

Few of those who had made such encouraging noises actually showed up when they scattered Edric's ashes. It was difficult to blame them. His widow had chosen a damp, granite cold February morning to set his mortal remains free in the valley they had both loved so much. As the grim, black-clad cortege slowly trudged and squelched its way across the campsite, over the footbridge and alongside the stream that cut through the foot of the valley, some of those few wished that they had come up with excuses of their own.

The beauty of the valley was impossible to deny, but February was doing its best to hide it. A cold mist was concealing the peaks of the surrounding hills so that only the immediate inclines on each side of the stream could be seen at all. The sheep all scattered at the approach of the mourners, all except one whose spinal column protruded from its fur mat, and whose gaping skull lay immobile, gazing blindly forever at the hidden sky. That a dead sheep lay no more that several feet from the spot where Edric was to be scattered was seen as a bad omen by most of the entourage, many of whom had given up trying to keep shoes and trousers clean, and instead hoped to get this ceremony over with as quickly as possible and retreat forthwith to the Ragleth Inn.

# Melpomene

Edric's widow was unperturbed. She and Edric had spent hours happily sitting by this stream, and her vision of the immediate environment owed more to the comforts of nostalgia than to the inhospitable reality of the day. She stood for a moment, bringing to mind some of her favoured memories of this place, and of the man she had discovered it with. And then, with a few secret, whispered valedictions he was gone. There was nothing dramatic about it once it had happened. Like so many little rituals, the drama was all in the minds of the actors, but for Edric's widow it was the fulfilment of a promise, and of Edric's final will. For her, the meaning was not in the moment but in the acceptance of a reality outside of time; of an eternal persistence of life, whose presence could best be caught in moments of forgetfulness, of forgetting who we are, and in wordless realisations that we may be something other than what we think we are.

She and Edric had talked a lot about such things, and where she had not quite fully understood, he understood for her. And where he had not quite fully believed, she believed for him. And so they had complemented each other, each providing for the other's shortcomings. And in the weeks of his absence she had needed to believe more strongly in the reality of the other reality, the eternal order. In her distress at losing him she found it easy to comfort herself with this belief. But in his absence she found it increasingly difficult to understand why she believed it. And in the absence of a partial understanding she developed a perfect

belief. This cold February morning was to be the fulfilment and seal of that belief.

She spoke to none of the others about these matters as they filed inelegantly back across the mud and moss to the warmth of the Inn, but she seemed to glow with an inner power that comforted her friends. They could see that this morning's ritual held deep meaning for her, even if it lacked the picturesque grandeur that they had been led to believe would accompany it. There was a sense of completion, a feeling of finality in the air.

There was great relief in being back at the inn. Tongues were readily loosened, with men offering to buy everyone drinks, and women fussing over the prepared food. There seemed little to say about the morning's ceremony as its icy grasp was thawed by the crackling log fire in the small pub lounge. This half of the inn had been set aside for the informal wake with a handwritten notice reading, 'Private function, please use other door for bar', stuck to the frosted glass of the door. And so the mourners remained untroubled by the few locals and visiting walkers who came to the pub.

Relatives who had not seen each other since the last funeral caught up with each other's news, and Edric's few friends who had turned up segregated themselves into a closed ring of drinkers and reminiscers. There was an air of awkward cordiality. Some of the relatives struck

up conversation with some of the friends, either about the food that was on offer, the location of the scattering, or the nature of relationship to Edric. Some of the men immediately intuited a resonance with each other and heartily exchanged anecdotes. It was mostly the women who sought to attend to Edric's widow's feelings. They surrounded her with a loose and informal confederation of allies who instinctively knew when to refer to her loss and when to distract her with practicalities. Everyone sensed that her dignified self-overcoming was entirely admirable, and felt glad to have come to this strange ritual; even if they did not understand its significance, the fact of its importance to Edric's widow was undeniable.

Little time passed before protracted and uncomfortable goodbyes were being presented to the widow. Her deportment and mien throughout were flawless; she was noble. As each exiting party left, the lounge became a quieter and more reflective place. The general background noise of chatter disappeared and everyone became more self-conscious, as their words could be heard by everyone else. The women were less affected by this than the men. No one was surprised when Edric's widow escaped to the Ladies' for a few moments. As she entered the toilet, she was stunned to hear an alien, disembodied voice talking to her. She was already in a sensitive frame of mind, so she felt resigned to this strange experience, and let it happen with a sense of resignation. The voice was confused but it spoke of the reality of death, and its primacy.

# Melpomene

As those moments of her absence grew to long minutes, no one worried. After ten minutes, one of the women discreetly went to see if she was okay. Her confused return to the lounge, trying to stifle her panic with a fear of being accused of overreaction, alerted the mourners to the fact that something was wrong.

When the men broke the toilet door open they found her seated fully clothed on the toilet lid, her hands clasped in her lap, and her face a mask of quiet contentment. Although they were able to stop the blood flow from her wrists she had already lost too much, and Edric's widow was pronounced dead on arrival at the hospital.

There was little that could profitably be said about the sad events of that January and February, though much actually was said behind closed doors. Edric and his widow had died childless, so there was nothing left to stifle unanswerable questions. Those who had been present at the scattering of Edric's ashes seemed to be most obviously affected by this further tragedy; some even spoke of their feelings to a reporter who subsequently wrote a short piece for the local newspaper. But the effects of Edric's widow's shocking suicide went much further, and much deeper.

Of those who had not, for whatever reason, attended the scattering of Edric's ashes, there was a great deal of confusion and hurt. Many thought that Edric's widow would not have done what she did if only they had been

there. These bereaved felt a mixture of anger and guilt, and often could not distinguish between the two: if only I had been there, she would still be alive because I would have sensed that something was wrong, so why didn't anyone else spot it? Over time, as the Earth thawed and then froze again, the energy that animated such complex emotions dissipated itself.

There were others who were affected by the suicide who did not think that it would have been prevented if they had had an opportunity to intervene. They accepted a much more fatalistic interpretation of those sad events, and believed that there must have been a power that possessed Edric's widow, a force invoked through her grief that had been the real motivation lying behind her actions. They accepted that her suicide was inevitable because they didn't believe that she was truly responsible for it.

Of these fatalists, some few who were of a pre-existing melancholy temperament came to feel that there was in any case a degree of inevitability to suicide. Not that they were drawn to suicide themselves, but they saw that death held such power, such a ubiquitous horror, that it was understandable that some would be overwhelmed it.

One of those so affected was an old friend of Edric's who had maintained only sporadic contact with him since his marriage, and that mostly conducted through third parties. This friend had suffered in the past from a series

of violently terrifying nightmares which usually left him lying awake in the middle of the night, soaked in sweat, and focussed quite clearly on the reality of the inevitability of death. Following each nightmare, his fear and morbidity would recede as the sun rose, so that by the time he started work his only problem was a lingering tiredness; the perception brought about by the nightmare was forgotten.

A few days after Edric's widow had killed herself this friend was visited by another of his terrifying nightmares. He was quite unprepared for it, as he had not suffered from one for some years previously. In the dream he was sitting in a bar with the mourners following the scattering of Edric's ashes. In the strange manner of dreams, he was both a detached observer and an intimate confidante of Edric's widow, hearing her innermost thoughts. He watched, and heard, as she stood up from the table and made her way to the Ladies' toilet, thinking to herself about her imminent death. She was consumed with the idea that she would soon be reunited with her husband, inhabiting the same nether universe that Edric was in. He tried to reason with her, to talk her out of her set course. He explained to her that she could not be reunited with Edric because 'Edric' no longer existed. There was no Heaven, or any other afterlife for him to go to. He had died and therefore no longer existed. He pleaded with her not to go through with her suicide, as it could only lead to a complete absence of being, and that was the most terrifying thing in the world. She refused to shift her focus from her imminent suicide, and cut her

wrists open as she smiled at him. She waited to die, to meet Edric again, but she simply disappeared from view, certainly to nothingness. At this point in the nightmare, he realised that Edric's widow had disappeared completely from existence, and that he, at some point, would also certainly disappear from existence. He was now trapped in the toilet cubicle alone and he felt an overwhelming sense of emptiness surrounding him. He realised that an eternity of this emptiness, however horrifying, would at least be a form of existence, and when he thought about the reality of the absence of existence, the total annihilation of self, he awoke, breathless and panicked.

As with previous nightmares throughout his life, the sun expelled the terror and allowed him to continue with his day. When he returned home from work that evening his wife and daughter were both sitting in the garden listening to the radio in the sun. He looked at them with overwhelming love and suddenly remembered the feeling in his dream, or rather, the absence of feeling, the absence of everything. He stared at his wife and daughter and started to hear some of the voices from the dream. He wondered how he could reconcile his love for his wife and daughter with the knowledge of their certain deaths. He poured water into a glass and tried to forget about it.